NOT THAT PET!

Smriti Halls   Rosalind Beardshaw

WALKER BOOKS
AND SUBSIDIARIES
LONDON • BOSTON • SYDNEY • AUCKLAND

For Mabel, Isaac, Eli & Joey ... and your
fabulous mum and dad – S.P-H. x

To Freddie and Iris with all my love x – R.B.

First published 2021 by Walker Books Ltd, 87 Vauxhall Walk, London SE11 5HJ • Text © 2021 Smriti Prasadam-Halls • Illustrations © 2021 Rosalind Beardshaw
The right of Smriti Prasadam-Halls and Rosalind Beardshaw to be identified as the author and illustrator respectively of this work has been asserted by them in accordance with the Copyright, Designs and Patents Act 1988 • This book has been typeset in Alice • Printed in China • All rights reserved. No part of this book may be reproduced, transmitted or stored in an information retrieval system in any form or by any means, graphic, electronic or mechanical, including photocopying, taping and recording, without prior written permission from the publisher. • British Library Cataloguing in Publication Data: a catalogue record for this book is available from the British Library • ISBN 978-1-4063-8789-6 • www.walker.co.uk • 10 9 8 7 6 5 4 3 2 1

Mabel's family were picking a pet.

"Mabel!" said Mum. "YOU choose which to get."

"*YIPPEE!*" said Mabel, and she chose ...

AN ELEPHANT!

for Mabel & family

He gave the best hugs!

He gave the best rides!

With upside-down lifts
and down-the-trunk slides.

He worked in the garden and planted the seeds,
he watered the flowers and pulled up the weeds. BUT ...

he trampled the roses and stood on the plums,
and squashed Mabel's strawberries
and sat on ...

her **MUM!**

And Mabel's mum squeaked,

"NOT THAT PET!

Choose something SMALLER!"

So Mabel chose ...

ANTS!

The ants were so busy,
they marched here and there,

they marched
through the kitchen,

they marched
up the stairs.

They marched round the bedroom ...

they marched down the wall ...

and soon they got lost ... for they were so SMALL!

Then Mabel's dad started jiggling,
for those naughty ants ...
had marched their way into
his UNDERPANTS!

And Mabel's dad giggled,

"NOT THAT PET!

Choose something we can SEE!"

So Mabel chose ...

A SKUNK!

With black-and-white stripes,
she thought THIS
will be
right.

They could see him by day.

They could see him by night.

He had soft, silky fur and a nose pink and wet.
There was simply no doubt that she'd got the best pet.

BUT ...

The Baby surprised him by giving a yell ...
and that skunk went and made
the most TERRIBLE SMELL!

And they ALL held their noses
and gasped, "NOT THAT PET!
Choose something that's
NOT AFRAID of The Baby!"

So Mabel chose ...

A SNAKE!

Her coat was bright silver
with patches of gold,
extremely exotic
but wiggly to hold.

And *she* wasn't scared,
no, that much was true.

Quite quickly she caused a right hullabaloo!

She slinked and she slithered with barely a sound,

Sssssss ... she coiled herself round ...

and around ...

until Grandad spluttered,

"NOT THAT PET!

Choose something with LEGS!"

So Mabel chose ...

A SPIDER!

They all took one look and screeched,

"NO! THERE'S NO WAY!"

From the top of the chair they yelled,

"TAKE IT AWAY!"

"OK then," said Mabel, "well what about these?
You know I'll look after them...
PLEASE, *pretty* please?"

But the worms were
too wriggly,

the hyena
too giggly,

the bear was
too growly,

the wolf was
too howly.

The hedgehog was much too prickly to touch,

the rabbit so shy that it stayed in its hutch.

The leopard leapt out and gave Grandma a fright,

and the owl kept on hooting, the whole of the night.

Mabel almost gave up.

She said, "No, it's no use. There isn't a pet
that's the right one to choose!"

But then she thought ...
I just need to pick something FURRY and SWEET.

Without lots of legs
or gigantic great feet.

Nothing too smelly
and nothing too tiny.

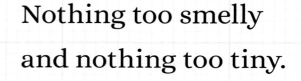

Nothing too scaly
and nothing too spiny.

Not noisy or scary or
covered in spikes.

I'll choose something friendly
that EVERYONE likes.

A pet that will like to curl up for a nap,
a pet that's just happy to sit on your lap,
a pet you can cuddle and snuggle and pat...

"I'VE GOT IT!" she yelled. And she chose ...

A RAT!